To our talented family:
Mom and Dad, Devin and Sarah,
Larissa, Paul, and Tanya

Special thanks to our
five-legged creature model,
and marble monster
extraordinaire, Kylie

SIMON & SCHUSTER BOOKS FOR YOUNG READERS • An imprint of Simon & Schuster Children's Publishing Division • 1230 Avenue of the Americas, New York, New York 10020 • © 2021 by Terry Fan and Eric Fan • Book design by Lizzy Bromley © 2021 by Simon & Schuster, Inc. • All rights reserved, including the right of reproduction in whole or in part in any form. • SIMON & SCHUSTER BOOKS FOR YOUNG READERS and related marks are trademarks of Simon & Schuster, Inc. • For information about special discounts for bulk purchases, please contact Simon & Schuster Special Sales at 1-866-506-1949 or business@simonandschuster.com. • The Simon & Schuster Speakers Bureau can bring authors to your live event. • For more information or to book an event, contact the Simon & Schuster Speakers Bureau at 1-866-248-3049 or visit our website at www.simonspeakers.com. • The text for this book was set in Bembo. • The illustrations for this book were rendered in graphite and then colored digitally. • Manufactured in China • 0621 SCP • First Edition • 2 4 6 8 10 9 7 5 3 1 • Library of Congress Cataloging-in-Publication Data • Names: Fan, Terry, author, illustrator. | Fan, Eric, author, illustrator. • Title: It fell from the sky / Terry Fan and Eric Fan. • Description: First edition. | New York : Simon & Schuster Books for Young Readers, 2021. | Audience: Ages 4-8. | Audience: Grades K-1. | Summary: All the insects agree that the object that fell from the sky is a Wonder, but when Spider decides it is his, he risks losing all of his friends. • Identifiers: LCCN 2020018462 (print) | LCCN 2020018463 (eBook) | ISBN 9781534457621 (hardcover) | ISBN 9781534457638 (eBook) • Subjects: CYAC: Spiders—Fiction. | Insects—Fiction. | Sharing—Fiction. | Friendship—Fiction. • Classification: LCC PZ7.1.F3542 It 2021 (print) | LCC PZ7.1.F3542 (eBook) | DDC [E]-dc23 • LC record available at https://lccn.loc.gov/2020018462 • LC eBook record available at https://lccn.loc.gov/2020018463

JJ
FAN
TERRY

IT FELL FROM THE SKY

THE FAN BROTHERS

SIMON & SCHUSTER BOOKS FOR YOUNG READERS
New York   London   Toronto   Sydney   New Delhi

WEST HARTFORD
PUBLIC LIBRARY
8376

It fell from the sky on a Thursday.

Ladybug was perched on a leaf when it landed. "I had a very good view. It bounced three times, then rolled to a stop," she said. The Inchworm insisted it only bounced twice. Everyone agreed it was the most amazing thing they had ever seen.

"Remarkable," said the Walking Stick.
He was happy to find something even
stranger than himself in the garden.

A Frog assumed it was a gumdrop.
He didn't like how it tasted.

The Dung Beetle tried to
roll it, but it was too heavy.

The Stinkbug doubted that
it fell from the sky at all.
He thought it might have
grown from the ground,
like a flower.

Finally, the wise Grasshopper was consulted.
"It is not of earthly origins," he concluded.
"Most likely a fallen star, a comet,
or perhaps even a small planet."

The Luna Moth knew it was
not a comet or a star or a planet.
It was a magical chrysalis that
needed to be kept warm.

She waited all through the night,
but the chrysalis never hatched.

In the morning, there was another surprise. "I think we can all agree that whatever it is, it most certainly belongs to me," said the crafty Spider. "After all, it fell right into my web."

Nobody remembered the web
being there the day before, but,
in fairness, nobody remembered
it *not* being there either.

Spider gathered everyone around so they could hear his plan. He would build a Grand Exhibit to properly show off the Wonder from the Sky.

Construction took many weeks, but when WonderVille finally opened, everyone agreed it had been worth the effort.

Even when the Spider explained tickets would cost
one leaf apiece, it seemed like a fair enough price.

Visitors came from far and wide. WonderVille was even more wondrous at night, thanks to the Fireflies hired to light up the display. The lines were long, so the Spider smartly raised the ticket price. Only a few insects grumbled.

But as the lines grew longer,
and the price grew higher . . .
the grumbles grew louder.

The Spider just hurried
customers through his exhibit.
What was there to grumble about?
He was giving them a rare glimpse
of the Wonder from the Sky!

Soon the Spider was wealthy beyond imagination.

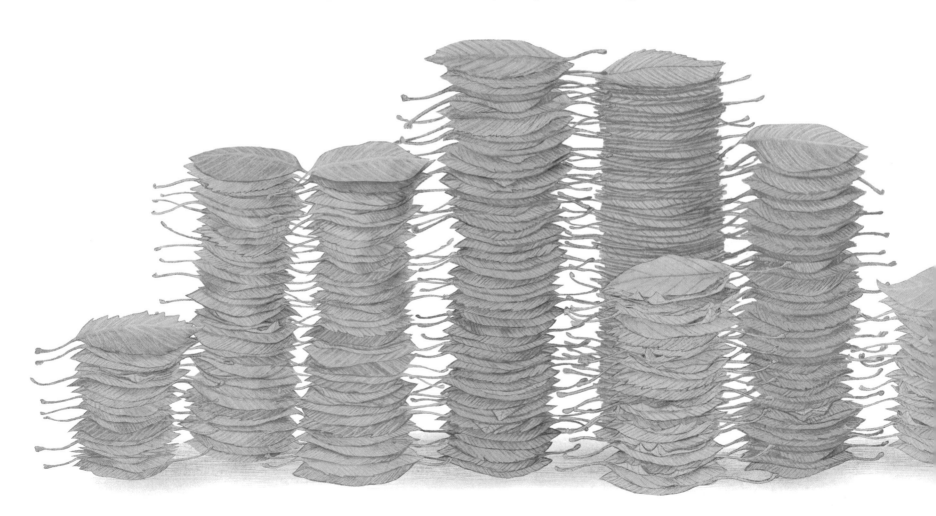

But where had everyone gone?
The Spider assumed they must have left to spread the word about how wonderful WonderVille was. Brand-new customers would arrive!

But that was before the Unexpected Disaster.

A five-legged creature stole the Wonder
and took it back to the sky.

The Spider was all alone.
There was no one to help him rebuild.

In the weeks that followed, some of
the insects returned to the garden.
Flowers grew back, and the long grass
covered the flattened anthills.

No one paid Spider much mind.
It was as if WonderVille never existed.

The night, as it sometimes does, shared a secret.

He gazed up at the sky and the stars shone down.

They didn't hide their light from anyone.

Not even a selfish Spider.

He knew what he needed to do.

Luckily, there is no creature
more patient than a spider.

High up in the flowers, he spun and spun.

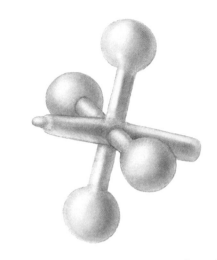

And sure enough, more
Wonders fell from the sky.

Everyone agreed it was the most
amazing thing they had ever seen.

Especially the Spider.